THE MAGIC FISH

Text by Maria Francesca Gagliardi
Illustrated by Štěpán Zavřel

MACDONALD : LONDON

On a faraway seacoast stands an ancient city where, everyday,
ships sail past houses, palaces, gardens, and a great museum.
In that museum are many paintings by famous artists.

There is one painting in the museum that all children specially love. It is of a Magic Golden Fish which seems to float, without moving, against a deep blue background. Whenever children visit the museum they stand for a long time and look at the Magic Fish.

Sometimes, when the Museum Attendant looks the other way, a child puts out his hand to touch the Fish. Then the Fish opens its big round eye and smiles at him. And the goldfish in the little fountain in the museum gallery, murmur: "Do you think he would come and play with us?" One day an attendant took down the painting, so as to clean the wall behind it. He placed the painting against the fountain. The goldfish were delighted and called: "Hello! Magic Fish!"

At first it seemed as if the Magic Fish had not heard. But the goldfish called again and again: "Magic Fish! Magic Fish! Come and play!" Suddenly the Magic Fish began to gleam and ripple. Then he jumped right out of the picture and into the fountain. There he dived and wriggled his way to the bottom where he found the hole by which water came in from the sea. "Follow me, friends!" he shouted. "Quickly, quickly!" All the goldfish followed him at once. By the time the guards noticed the Magic Fish was gone, he and the goldfish were miles away.

The fish found their way beneath the big city and swam and swam until they came to the open sea. Their eyes grew bigger and bigger. All around them they saw seaweed, rock, coral, sea anemones, jellyfish and mussels. Fish of all sorts and shapes darted around them on their morning swim.

Then three turtles swam slowly up to the newcomers. They bowed politely and said: "Welcome in the name of all the Seafolk! A hearty welcome to you!" The Magic Fish answered: "Thank you for your kind welcome, friends! Allow me to dance for you." And at once he began to dance. His movements were so beautiful, that all the fish in the clear water around him stopped and held their breath as they watched.

Suddenly an enormous shadow darkened the water. A great net came floating down from above. Before they knew what was happening they were all caught in it.

The fishermen in the boat above shouted: "Heave, Heave!" as they pulled in the net with its heavy catch of fish.
Luckily, however, the Magic Fish was among the poor captives. In the sunlight he gleamed golden bright. "I must help my friends at once," he thought. Then he darted about with such speed that he dazzled the fishermen's eyes with the reflected rays of the sun, so that they let go of the net in their fright. Slowly the great net opened and out swam all the fish led by their friend, the Magic Fish.

All the Seafolk, fish, crabs and turtles thought the Magic Fish a hero. "How brave he is!" they said, "How clever!"

They were so grateful that the turtles now bowed twice before him and the squid sang a special song for him.

But there was one little fish who did not join in these praises. He swam sadly up to the Magic Fish and said:"I have a friend who is a prisoner in the cave of an octopus. He cannot escape because this octopus never sleeps, but guards his cave day and night. Can you think of any way to help my poor friend?"

"Let us go and have a look," said the Magic Fish.

Completely unafraid, the Magic Fish swam towards the cave. There he found the octopus who had not slept for a hundred years. The octopus goggled at the bold invader, and as soon as the Magic Fish came near enough shot out one of his long arms, as quick as lightning, to catch him. But the Magic Fish moved even faster. He dashed out of reach and began to swim around and around the octopus, singing: "Sleep, octopus, sleep!" and all the time he glinted like a mirror with the sun on it. The octopus, as he tried to watch him, spun around like a top until he felt absolutely dizzy.

"Sleep, octopus, sleep!" sang the Magic Fish, and the octopus gave a great yawn. He could not keep his eyes open any longer; they closed, and his long arms hung limply down. Finally he fell asleep and snored. Then the Magic Fish called to the prisoner in a low voice: "Hello, friend! You can come out now! The octopus is asleep." And out came the little fish to race with the Magic Fish towards the freedom of the open sea.

But already another danger
threatened them. The crab who
acted as sentry cried: "Save
yourselves, all who can! The
swordfish is coming!" The fish were
very frightened, and swam off as
fast as they could. But where could
they hide from this fierce,
fast-moving enemy?

Already the great
sword was almost
touching the little
fish, who were all
so frightened that
now they dared
not move.

But at the last moment, the Magic
Fish shouted: "Courage my friends!
I will save you! Follow me!"

Then all of them darted behind him
through a narrow gap in the rocks
where the swordfish could not
follow. So, once again the Magic
Fish had saved his friends from
terrible danger.

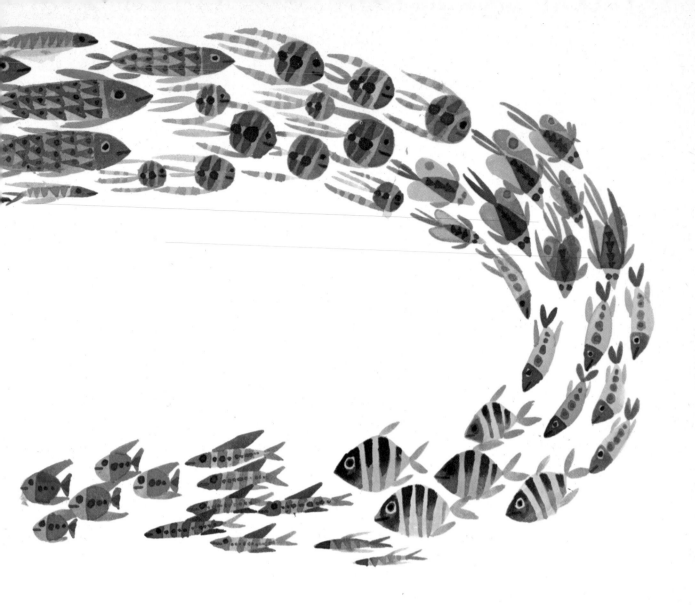

The Seafolk celebrated the rescue from the octopus with a wonderful party. Turtles and jellyfish, little fish and big fish, thick fish and thin fish, swam in circles around the Magic Fish. They all begged him to be their king.

"I cannot thank you enough for the offer," answered the Magic Fish. "But I am not sure whether I can accept. I am not a sea creature. I come from a painting in a museum, and I must go and see whether the children in the city still need me." Then all the fish accompanied him on his return journey under the city to the museum.

The Magic Fish soon found the pipe through which they had escaped, and the goldfish followed him back into the museum. For them the sea was too dangerous.

No-one saw the Magic Fish and the goldfish arrive back in the
fountain. The fish took a quick look round. Everything was still
the same, except that the children who used to watch the Magic
Fish now stood sadly in front of the empty picture. "He has
gone," they cried, "The beautiful fish has gone!" Then the
Magic Fish decided to go back into his picture. "That is my
place!" he said, "The sea fish will understand. The children have
always been my best friends. I cannot go away and leave them."

As it grew dark in the museum, and moonlight shone in through the windows, the Magic Fish said good-bye to the goldfish. Then with a flick of his tail he shot himself out of the fountain, high into the air and landed right in the middle of his picture.

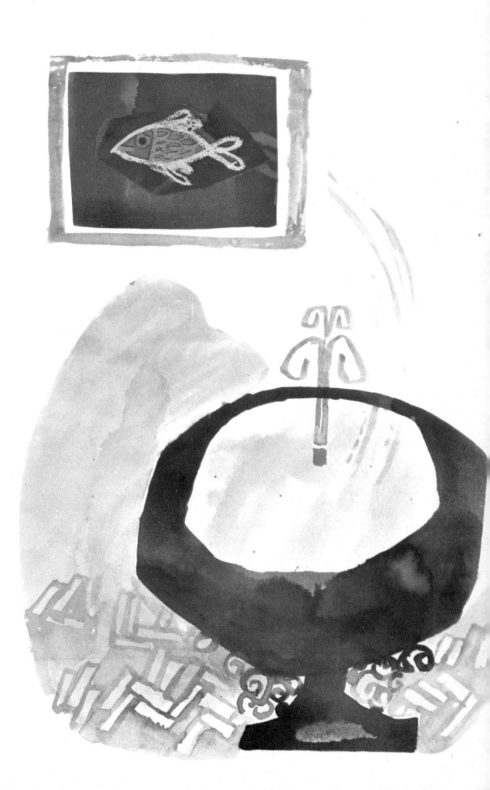

THE END